Old Mother Goose,
When she wanted to wander,
Would ride through the air,
On a very fine gander.

New Dada Geese,
When they want to wander,
Play around with old rhymes,
To make them goofy grander.

To Blanche Fisher Wright
JS & JR

First edition 2022

Library of Congress Catalog Card Number 2021953327
ISBN 978-0-7636-9434-0

22 23 24 25 26 27 APS 10 9 8 7 6 5 4 3 2 1

Printed in Humen, Dongguan, China

This book was typeset in Coldstyle.
The illustrations were done in mixed media.

Candlewick Press
99 Dover Street
Somerville, Massachusetts 02144

www.candlewick.com

THE REAL
DADA
MOTHER
GOOSE

Illustrated by
Blanche Fisher Wright

A Treasury of Complete Nonsense

JON SCIESZKA

illustrated by

JULIA ROTHMAN

CANDLEWICK PRESS

CONTENTS

MORE Humpty Dumpty**S**

Jack**S** Be Nimble

OTHER Mother Hubbard**S**

Hey Diddle Diddle DIDDLE DIDDLE DIDDLE DIDDLE

Hickory 6 Dickory DockS

Twinkle Twinkle TWINKLE TWINKLE TWINKLE TWINKLE Little Star

NEVER END

NOTES

MORE NOTES

MORE HUMPTY DUMPTYS

Humpty Dumpty sat on a wall.
Humpty Dumpty had a great fall.
All the King's horses, and all
the King's men,
Cannot put Humpty together again.

So Dada Geese decided to help . . .

Humpty Dumpty sat on a ▮

Humpty Dumpty had a great ▮

All the King's ▮ and all

the King's ▮

Cannot put Humpty together ▮

DEFINITION

Humpty Dumpty sat on a continuous vertical brick or stone structure.

Humpty Dumpty had a great sudden uncontrollable descent.

All the King's solid-hoofed plant-eating domesticated mammals with flowing manes and tails, used for riding, racing, and to carry and pull loads,

And all the King's persons in military service and especially enlisted persons in the army,

Cannot put Humpty back in his previous position or condition again.

BORING

Humpty Dumpty
  sat in a chair.
Humpty Dumpty
  combed his one hair.
All the King's horses,
  and all the King's men,
Didn't really have
  to do anything.

POST CARD

Dear Mom and Dad,
Camp is going great.
Well, mostly great.
Yesterday I was sitting on a wall,
And there was a big whoosh of wind.
and I had a great fall.
And so far all the king's horses, and
all the king's men,
Haven't been able to put me
together again.
But swimming and camping have
been a lot of fun.
Love, Humpty

MoM + Dad Dumpty
18 Kingston Lane
Colchester, England
CO1 CO4

MORSE CODE

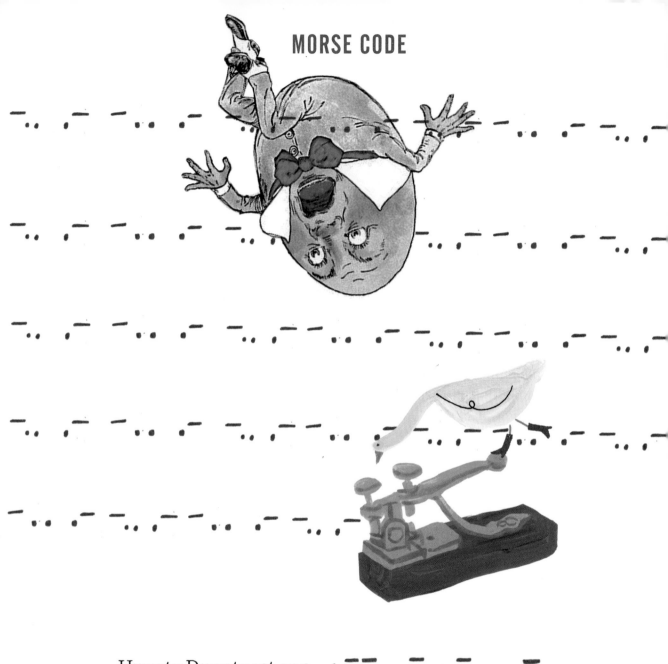

Humpty Dumpty sat on a

Humpty Dumpty had a great

All the King's horses, and all the
   King's men,

Cannot put Humpty together

6

COMPUTER TRANSLATION TELEPHONE

Humpty Dumpty sat on a wall.

Humpty Dumpty had a great fall.

All the King's horses,

   and all the King's men,

Cannot put Humpty together again.

ENGLISH → SPANISH

Humpty Dumpty se sentó en una pared.

Humpy Dumpty tuvo una gran caída.

Todos los caballos del Rey,

   y todos los hombres del Rey,

No puedo volver a armar a Humpty.

SPANISH → ARABIC

جلس هامبتي دمبتي على الحائط.
هامبتي دمبتي تعرض لسقوط كبير.
كل خيل الملك وكل رجال الملك،
لا يمكنني إعادة تجميع هامبتي.

ARABIC → CHINESE

胖蛋儿坐在墙上。
胖蛋儿摔倒了。
所有国王的马匹和所有国王的人马，
我无法重新组装 Humpty。

CHINESE → LATIN

Humpty Dumpty muro sedet.

Humpty Dumpty cecidit.

Omnes equi reges et omnes viri reges,

Humpty coeundi nequeo.

LATIN → ENGLISH

Humpty Dumpty sits on the wall.

Humpty Dumpty fell.

All horses are kings, and all men are kings;

I can't meddle with Humpty.

Jack be nimble.

Jack be quick.

Jack jump over the candlestick.

SECRET CODES

PIG LATIN:

Jack be imble-nay.

Jack be ick-quay.

Jack ump-jay over-yay the andlestick-cay.

BACKWARD:

Elbmin eb kcaj.

Kciuq eb kcaj.

Kcitseldnac eht revo pmuj kcaj.

REVERSE ALPHABET:

Qzxp yv mrnyov.

Qzxp yv jfrxp.

Qzxp qfnk levi gsv xzmwovhgrxp.

MULTIPLE CHOICE

(F) *please see me after class!*

Jack be

   a) nimble

X b) fizzle

   c) pickle

Jack be

X a) slick

   b) quick

   c) sick

Jack jump over the

   a) candlestick

   b) pile of brick

X c) hockey stick

13

ESPERANTO

Jack estu facilmova.

Jack rapidu.

Jack saltas super la kandelabron.

BAD LIB

Jack be _smelly_.
(adjective)

Jack be _green_.
(adjective 2)

Jack jump over the _jelly bean_.
(noun that rhymes with adjective 2)

Jack be _ugly_.
(adjective)

Jack be _sweaty_.
(adjective 2)

Jack jump over the _Abominable Yeti_.
(noun that rhymes with adjective 2)

Jack be _goofy_.
(adjective)

Jack be _funny_.
(adjective 2)

Jack jump over the _unbelievably huge Easter Bunny_.
(noun that rhymes with adjective 2)

Jack be _wrinkled_.
(adjective)

Jack be _teeny_.
(adjective 2)

Jack jump over the _steaming bowl of fettuccini_.
(noun that rhymes with adjective 2)

Nack be jimble.
Quack be jick.
Jack jump over the standlekick.

The main character in this nursery rhyme is Jack. There is also a burning candlestick. Jack is nimble. Jack is quick. Jack sees the candlestick, and jumps over it. While it is burning.

I liked this rhyme because there was some good action.

I did not like this rhyme because you don't really know what happened in the end. Like did Jack get burned? Did the candlestick get knocked over?

You will never know.

Old Mother Hubbard went to the cupboard,

To get her poor dog a bone.

But when she got there, the cupboard was bare.

And so the poor dog had none.

JABBERWOCKY

Old Mother Jabber went to the clabber,

To get her frum jub a gove.

But when she got wabe, the clabber was grabe.

And so the frum jub had tove.

RE-VERB

Old Mother Hubbard moseyed / progressed / skipped / hightailed it / took a hike to the cupboard,

To gain / grab / pick up / acquire / capture / fetch / snag / wrangle / procure / cop / bag her poor dog a bone.

But when she arrived / reached / turned up / blew in / popped up / dropped anchor there, the cupboard sat / existed / stood bare.

And so the poor dog gained / acquired / obtained / received / procured / took in / latched onto / got hold of none.

COMIC STRIP

REVERSE

None, had the poor dog, just so.

Bare was the cupboard, when she got there.

A bone for her poor dog to get

From the cupboard, where went Old Mother Hubbard.

THE HUBBARD VARIATIONS

Old Mother Hubbard went to the cupboard,

To get her poor dog a bone.

But when she got there, the cupboard was bare.

And so the poor dog ate the cat food.

3/100

Old Mother Luvven went to the oven,

To get her poor iguana some crickets and mealworms.

But when she got there, the oven was bare.

And so the poor iguana had kale and parsley.

56/100

Young Dr. Fabratory went to the laboratory,
To refit her latest robot with a new, faster, and larger memory.
But when she got there, the laboratory had vanished.
And so Dr. Fabratory and her robot were left to ponder (1) the
possibility of this world being nothing but a game played
by a more developed consciousness, and (2) the resulting essential
meaninglessness of life as we know it.

78/100

IF U CN RD THS

OLD MTHR HBRD WNT TO TH CPBRD,
TO GT HER PR DOG A BN.
BT WHN SHE GT THR, TH CPBRD WS BR.
AND SO TH PR DOG HD NON.

HEY
DIDDLE
DIDDLE
DIDDLE
DIDDLE
diddle
DIDDLE

Hey diddle diddle, the cat and the fiddle.

The cow jumped over the moon.

The little dog laughed to see such sport.

And the dish ran away with the spoon.

DAILY GOOSE

Cow Jumps Moon, Dish Runs Away With Spoon

At 11:15 pm last night in the pasture behind the Old Woman's Shoe, local resident Ms. Cow was so startled by a Cat playing a Fiddle that she jumped over the Moon.

"Never seen such a sight," said a Little Dog who observed the giant leap. "It was crazy, I just had to laugh."

Three Men in a Tub — the Butcher, the Baker, the Candlestick maker — also reported seeing dinnerware running away from the scene.

Neither Ms. Dish nor Mr. Spoon could be reached for comment.

Hey Diddle Diddle Stew

Ingredients:
1 cat
1 fiddle
1 cow
1 moon
1 dog (little)

Prep Time: 20 min
Cook Time: 17 min

Serves 6-12

Directions:

Assemble all ingredients. Give cat fiddle. Stir in cow to jump over moon. Wait for dog to laugh. Mix dish until it runs away with spoon.

Serve using any dinnerware left.

JOKE

HAIKU

Hey diddle diddle,

Cat fiddles, cow moons, dog laughs.

"Run!" says Dish to Spoon.

POP QUIZ

Name _____

1. Who is playing the fiddle?

2. What is the cow jumping over?

3. Where did the dog get that clown outfit?

4. When did the dog laugh?

5. Why do you think the dish is running away with the spoon?

6. How much do these reading quizzes make you want to run away with the spoon?

HICKORY 6
DICKORY
DOCKS

Hickory, dickory, dock.

The mouse ran up the clock.

The clock struck one,

And down he run.

Hickory, dickory, dock.

EGYPTIAN HIEROGLYPHS

Hickory, dickory,

The mouse ran up the

The clock struck

And down he

Hickory, dickory,

Hickory, dickory, dolphin.
The muffin ran up the cloud.
The cloud struck one,
And down the heart run.
Hickory, dickory, dolphin.

*Replace each noun and pronoun with the
seventh noun following it in the dictionary.

CROSSWORD PUZZLE

A, E, I, O, U . . . AND SOMETIMES Y

A

Hickory, dickory, dack.

The mouse jumped in a sack.

E

Hickory, dickory, deek.

The mouse dove in the creek.

I

Hickory, dickory, dike.

The mouse took Mary's bike.

O

Hickory, dickory, doke.

The mouse blew clouds of smoke.

U

Hickory, dickory, duck.

The mouse stepped in the muck.

Y

Hickory, dickory, dye.

The mouse began to fly.

ALL HOURS

 Hickory, dickory, dock.
The mouse ran up the clock.

 The clock struck seven,
Called up Kevin.

 The clock struck one,
And down he run.

 The clock struck eight,
He smashed a plate.

 The clock struck two,
He turned bright blue.

 The clock struck nine,
He swung a vine.

 The clock struck three,
Afternoon tea.

 The clock struck ten,
ESPN.

The clock struck four,
He gave a roar.

The clock struck eleven,
He went to heaven.

 The clock struck five,
He took a dive.

 The clock struck six,
He picked up sticks.

 The clock struck twelve,
And he couldn't think
of anything good that
rhymed with twelve
so he went to sleep.

MASH-UP

Hickory, dickory, dock.

Twinkle, twinkle, little star.

The mouse ran up the clock.

How I wonder what you are.

The clock struck one.

Up above the world so high.

And down he run.

Like a diamond in the sky.

Hickory, dickory, dock.

How I wonder what you are.

TWINKLE TWINKLE LITTLE STAR

Twinkle, twinkle, little star.

How I wonder what you are.

Up above the world so high,

Like a diamond in the sky.

Twinkle, twinkle, little star.

How I wonder what you are.

Twinkle, twinkle, little star.

Now we know just **what you are**.

A luminous ball of gas, mostly hydrogen and helium,
 held together by your own gravity, producing light
 and heat from nuclear fusion reactions in your core.

Twinkle, twinkle, little star.

Now we know just **what you are**.

ANAGRAM

WET LINK, WET LINK, little RATS.

How I DOWNER what you are.

Up above the DR. OWL so high,

Like a MAD ODIN in the sky.

WET LINK, WET LINK, little RATS.

How I DOWNER what you are.

REBUS

T + 😉 +L, T + 😉 +L, LITTLE ⭐.

HOW 👁 1 + DER WHAT **U R.**

UP AB + 🕊 − D THE 🌍 SO 👋,

L + 👁 +K A 💎 IN THE ☁☀☁.

T + 😉 +L, T + 😉 +L, LITTLE ⭐.

HOW 👁 1 + DER WHAT **U R.**

MUSICAL NOTATION

MILITARY ALPHABET

Twinkle, twinkle, little Sierra Tango Alpha Romeo.

How I wonder what you Alpha Romeo Echo.

Up above the Whiskey Oscar Romeo Lima Delta so high,

Like a Delta India Alpha Mike Oscar November Delta in the sky.

Twinkle, twinkle, little Sierra Tango Alpha Romeo.

How I wonder what you Alpha Romeo Echo.

SIMILE EXCESSIVELY

Twinkle, twinkle, little star,
How I wonder what you are.
Up above the world so high,
Like a diamond in the sky.

Like a slice of cherry pie.
Like a rug hung out to dry.
Like a humming tsetse fly.
Like a smoking dragon sigh.

Like a red-and-white-striped tie.
Like a stick poked in your eye.
Like angels we have heard on high.
Like fractions you must simplify.

$$\frac{63}{48} =$$

$$\frac{46829}{10,4628}$$

$$\frac{3}{4} = 0.75$$

$$\frac{12}{30} = \frac{2}{5}$$

$$\frac{10}{40} =$$

$$\frac{12}{42} =$$

Like a jazz bebop hi-fi.
Like a dream, I'll tell you why.
Like Bombay, now called Mumbai.
Like a gentle lullaby.

Like a glass to magnify.
Like a door's electric eye.
Like the country Uruguay.
Like those dumplings called shumai.

Like that old sweet by-and-by.
Like a fox quite on the sly.
Like John Adams Junior High.
Like those twins called Gemini.

Like your socks hung to drip-dry.
Like when I just say, "Bye-bye."
Like the Giant's "Fe Fo Fi."
Like the threat to do or die.

Like some kid you terrify.
Like a rhyme that's gone awry.
Like a scream "Oh me, oh my!"
. . .

Twinkle, twinkle, little star.
Please no more of what you are.

53

~~NEVER~~ THE END

Humpty Dumpty sat on a wall.

Jack jumped over the candlestick.

Old Mother Hubbard
went to the cupboard.

The dish ran away with the spoon.

Twinkle, twinkle, little star.

The mouse ran up the clock.

Little Bo Peep has lost her sheep.

Jack and Jill went up the hill.

One, two, buckle my shoe.
Now YOU make these old rhymes new.

Dada Geese writers! Dada Geese friends!
YOU put Humpty together again!

And **AGAIN** and **AGAIN** and
AGAIN and **AGAI**

Once upon a time...

Notes

Morse Code

Morse code is a system of communication using dashes and dots to represent each letter of the alphabet. It was named after Samuel Morse, inventor of the telegraph, and was first used around 1844, with pulses transmitting on a telegraph wire.

Morse code can also be transmitted as taps on a wall, audio tones (like honking your horn), or flashes of light. The code is spoken as "dah" for dashes, "dit" for dots.

While Morse code is no longer in use in international shipping, SOS is still a standard emergency distress signal. In Morse code, it is: . . . − − − . . .

Using Morse code, you can secretly write (and send) anything you can spell.

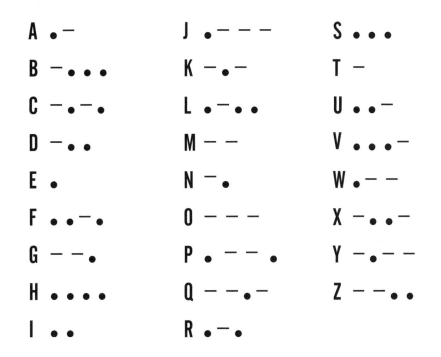

A .−   J .− − −   S . . .
B −. . .   K −.−   T −
C −.−.   L .−. .   U . .−
D −. .   M − −   V . . .−
E .   N −.   W .− −
F . .−.   O − − −   X −. .−
G − −.   P .− − .   Y −.− −
H . . . .   Q − −.−   Z − −. .
I . .   R .−.

Computer Translation Telephone

Telephone is a game played by a group of people in a line or circle.

The first person whispers a phrase to the person next to them.

That person whispers what they think they heard to the next person. Then that person whispers what they think they heard to the next person.

When the phrase has been whispered to the last person, they say out loud what they have heard.

And it is always amazing how much the phrase gets messed up.

Dada Computer Translation Telephone is played by typing a nursery rhyme into a computer translation program, then directing the computer to translate from one language to another to another to another . . . and finally back to the language you started in.

You might think computers would be very accurate at translating.

They are not.

Computers are, in fact, really bad (but often very funny) at translating.

The game of Telephone has many different names, including Gossip and Grapevine, and is played all over the world.

It is called *Stille Post* (Silent Mail) in Germany, *Telefon Rosak* (Broken Telephone) in Malaysia, and *Kulaktan Kulaga* (From Ear to Ear) in Turkey.

Esperanto

Esperanto is a language invented in 1887 by Ludwik Lejzer "L.L." Zamenhof.

He was a Polish ophthalmologist (eye doctor).

Zamenhof created Esperanto in the hopes it would save people time from learning a lot of different languages and become a shared universal language that would bring people from different countries together.

Winnie-the-Pooh, The Wonderful Wizard of Oz, and *Alice's Adventures in Wonderland* have all been translated into Esperanto.

Ask for them at your local library as *Winnie-La-Pu, La Mirinda Sorĉisto de Oz,* and *La Aventuroj de Alico en Mirlando.*

In Esperanto, *The Stinky Cheese Man* is *La Fetora Fromaĝo-Viro.*
Esperanto is fun, and easy to learn.

Hello	*Saluton*
Goodbye	*Adiaŭ*
How are you?	*Kiel vi fartas?*
I am fine.	*Mi fartas bone.*
Who farted?	*Kiu furzis?*
Not me!	*Ne mi!*
Can you say "poop" in Esperanto?	*Ĉu vi povas diri "kako" en Esperanto?*
Yes, you can.	*Jes, vi povas.*
Fantastic! Thanks.	*Mirinda! Dankon.*

Secret Codes

Codes are a good way to disguise information or hide text.

There are thousands of codes. Here are three handy ones:

PIG LATIN

It's not Latin. But it does sound like another language.
Change words by:

(1) taking the first letter/sound of every word

(2) adding –*ay* to it

(3) then moving that sound to the end of the word to
make a whole new word

pig	becomes	*ig-pay*
latin	becomes	*atin-lay*
you	becomes	*ou-yay*
me	becomes	*e-may*
she	becomes	*e-shay*
clam	becomes	*am-clay*

If the first letter of the word is a vowel:

– leave the word as it is

– just add –*yay* to the end

up	becomes	*up-yay*
over	becomes	*over-yay*
under	becomes	*under-yay*
old	becomes	*old-yay*

Meet me under the old clam.

becomes

Eet-may   e-may   under-yay   e-thay   old-yay   am-clay.

BACKWARD

Very easy to create but tricky to solve if you don't know the code.

Spell the entire message backward.

SEE TOM RUN! becomes *NUR MOT EES!*

REVERSE ALPHABET

Another very simple code that is tricky if you don't know it. Replace each letter with its matching letter in a reversed alphabet.

A B C D E F G H I J K L M N O P Q R S T U V W X Y Z
Z Y X W V U T S R Q P O N M L K J I H G F E D C B A

SEE TOM RUN! becomes *HVV GLN IFM!*

Spoonerism

Spoonerisms are words or phrases in which letters or syllables get switched, creating new, often funny words and phrases.

They are named after William Archibald Spooner, a British clergyman and teacher who lived from 1844 to 1930. He was a nervous speaker who would accidentally turn phrases like "a crushing blow" into "a blushing crow."

Reverend Spooner became so well known for mangling words in this way that by 1900, people were calling these mistakes spoonerisms.

Here are a few examples:

It's raining *dats and cogs*. (cats and dogs)
Memorize your *welling spurds*. (spelling words)
Comb your hair and *know your blows*. (blow your nose)
And don't forget to *shake a tower*. (take a shower)

Jabberwocky

"Jabberwocky" is a nonsense poem written by Charles Lutwidge Dodgson (better known by his pen name, Lewis Carroll). It appears in his book *Through the Looking-Glass, and What Alice Found There*, which was published in 1871. "Jabberwocky" uses invented words that sound like real words in English.

It begins:

'Twas brillig, and the slithy toves
Did gyre and gimble in the wabe.

In the book, Humpty Dumpty explains to Alice what the nonsense words mean. But you can probably come up with better guesses. And you can definitely make up your own nonsense words.

Haiku

Haiku is a type of short poem that originated in Japan.

In Japanese, it is written in three lines, with five syllables in the first line, seven in the second line, and five in the third.

Haiku is more than just a kind of poetry.

It is a way of seeing the very essence of existence.

Matsuo Bashō (1644–1694) was the first to use haiku as a separate form in itself.

> *Temple bells die out.*
> *The fragrant blossoms remain.*
> *A perfect evening!*

N + 7

N + 7 is a way to change any text into a completely new text. You replace each noun in a text with the seventh noun following it in a dictionary.

N + 7 was invented by a French fellow named Jean Lescure. Mr. Lescure was a poet and a member of a very interesting group of writers and mathematicians who called themselves Oulipo. *Oulipo* is short for *Ouvroir de littérature potentielle,* which in English means "workshop of potential literature." Founded on November 24, 1960, the Oulipo group likes to make new works by using different invented writing rules.

Raymond Queneau was one of the founders of Oulipo. *The Real Dada Mother Goose* is a tribute to an Oulipo book Mr. Queneau wrote called *Exercises in Style,* which tells the simple story of a man's bus trip . . . ninety-nine different ways.

Egyptian Hieroglyphs

Egyptian hieroglyphs were a writing system in ancient Egypt that used pictures to represent spoken sounds.

These hieroglyphs included pictures of animals (a lion, an owl), everyday objects (a basket, reeds), and some symbols (mouth, water).

Here is a simplified alphabet that shows which pictures stood for which sounds.

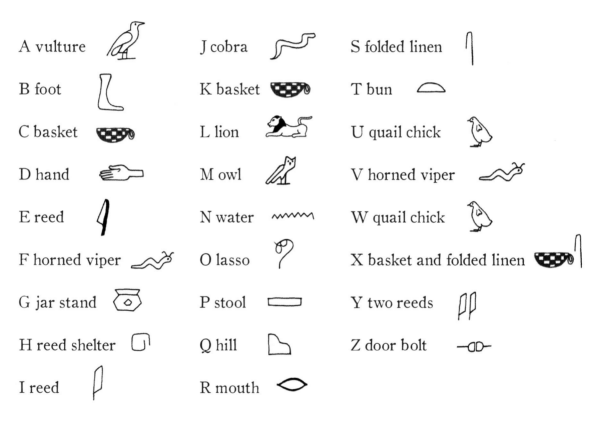

So *Jon* written in hieroglyphs is

Use this chart to write your name in hieroglyphs.
Amaze your friends! Annoy your enemies! Freak out your teachers!

Anagram

An anagram is made by rearranging the letters of a word or phrase to make a different word or phrase.

So STAR can be rearranged to spell RATS.

One anagram of JON SCIESZKA is IS SO JACK ZEN.

JULIA ROTHMAN anagrammed is HULA ARM JOINT.

ELIZABETH BICKNELL is HAZEL NIBBLE TICKLE.

AMY BERNIKER is REAMER BY INK.

CARTER HASEGAWA is AREA SCHWA GREAT.

DADA GEESE is A SAGE DEED.

Rebus

A rebus is a writing puzzle that uses pictures and letters to make words and phrases. Complicated rebuses add and subtract letters from pictured words. This kind of picture writing has been used for thousands of years.

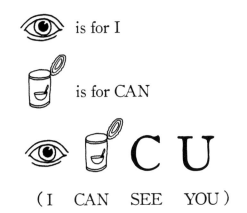

is for I

is for CAN

(I   CAN   SEE   YOU)

Musical Notation

Written music notes and symbols are a system for showing sound in a printed form.

The written word version of the first two lines of "Twinkle, Twinkle, Little Star" looks like this:

Twinkle, twinkle, little star.

How I wonder what you are.

The musical notation of the first two lines of the "Twinkle, Twinkle Little Star" song looks like this:

The musical notation for part of Claude Debussy's "Reverie" looks something like this:

"Twinkle, Twinkle, Little Star" is one of the few nursery rhymes we know the origin of. It was a poem written by the English author Jane Taylor and published in 1806 as "The Star."

This rhyme is probably so well known because by 1838 it was set to the music of an old French folk song, "Ah, vous dirai-je, Maman" ("Ah, Shall I Tell You, Mama"), a melody also used for "Baa, Baa, Black Sheep" and the alphabet song ("A-B-C-D-E-F-G").

Military Alphabet

You know how it is sometimes hard to understand someone on a phone? Especially when they are spelling a word? Like when you are spelling your name, and you say: "Yeah, it's spelled J-O-N."

And they say, "J-O-M?"

And you say, "No, J-O-NNNNNNN."

And they say, "MMMMM?"

And you say, "NOOO! NNNNNN!"

And they say, "You don't have to yell about it, Jom. Now, how do you spell *Shezzzka*?"

A spelling alphabet solves this problem.

Each of the twenty-six letters in the alphabet is given a distinct name.

You say the name assigned to each letter to avoid the confusion caused by a bad connection or pronunciation. *A* is *Alpha*, *B* is *Bravo*, *C* is *Charlie*, etc. To spell *JON*, you would then say, "That's *J* as in *Juliet*, *O* as in *Oscar*, and *N* as in *November*."

Spelling alphabets were invented in the early 1900s when people began using telephones and two-way radios. They became essential for wartime communications, and so they are commonly known as military alphabets.

The official name of the spelling alphabet used by most countries now is the International Radiotelephony Spelling Alphabet.

But try spelling *that* over the phone.

A Alpha	H Hotel	O Oscar	V Victor
B Bravo	I India	P Papa	W Whiskey
C Charlie	J Juliet	Q Quebec	X Xray
D Delta	K Kilo	R Romeo	Y Yankee
E Echo	L Lima	S Sierra	Z Zulu
F Foxtrot	M Mike	T Tango	
G Golf	N November	U Uniform	

More Notes

Mother Goose History

There may never have been an actual individual named Mother Goose.

Yes, there is a popular story that Mary Goose, buried in the old Granary Burying Ground in Boston in 1690, was the beloved old lady who invented these wonderful nursery rhymes and songs.

And other people swear that Elizabeth Foster Goose was the real Mother Goose . . . whose rhymes were published by her son-in-law in 1719.

But there is no evidence that Mary made up these nursery rhymes.

There is no copy of a 1719 book of Elizabeth's rhymes.

A hundred years earlier (in the 1600s in France), *mère l'oye* (Mother Goose) was a phrase used to describe a woman who told fun stories and rhymes to kids.

In 1697 a French writer named Charles Perrault published a collection of eight folktales called *Stories or Tales from Times Past, with Morals* with an added subtitle, *Tales of My Mother Goose.*

This is the earliest use of the words *Mother Goose* in print.

Then sometime around 1765, in England, the book company started by John Newbery published *Mother Goose's Melody.* Self-described as "The Most Celebrated Songs and Lullabies of the Old British Nurses," this book contained most of the rhymes we think of today as Mother Goose rhymes. And most publishers in the English-speaking world have used this collection as their source for Mother Goose books ever since.

So we will never know if there was one real Mother Goose.

But we do know that most of these Mother Goose rhymes have been around for a very long time, and that we are happy to be able to keep them around by re-telling, re-illustrating, and re-mixing them.

Blanche Fisher Wright

Blanche Fisher Wright illustrated the incredibly popular and wildly successful book *The Real Mother Goose*, first published in 1916.

She is almost as much a mystery as Mother Goose.

Ancestry records show she was born Blanche Viola Fisher on June 24, 1887, in Manitowoc, Wisconsin . . . and died January 16, 1971, in Illinois.

Blanche had a sister named Lola (two years younger) who became a Broadway actress.

She did have a brother named Charles Douglas (four years younger) who served in the US Army in World War I and invented toys.

By 1910, she had married Arthur Kendrick Wright in Milwaukee, Wisconsin.

On March 2, 1920, she married Charles Laite in New York City.

In 1925, Blanche and Charles adopted a baby and named him Gordon.

Gordon Laite grew up to illustrate children's books in the 1950s and 1960s.

And that's kind of all we know.

Blanche Fisher Wright's *The Real Mother Goose* has sold millions of copies.

Because the work of children's illustrators was not particularly valued in the 1900s, our record of what Blanche Fisher Wright published is incomplete. The following bibliography has been put together by collecting her books from sellers of old books.

We may never know much more about Blanche Fisher Wright Laite. But at least we have her illustrations and can imagine her through them.

A Blanche Fisher Wright Bibliography
(A Work-Still-in-Progress)

The Bye-lo series. Chicago: Rand McNally.

1913	*Hot Cross Buns and Other Mother Goose Rhymes*
1913	*Tommy Snooks and Other Mother Goose Rhymes*
1914	*Betty Blue and Other Mother Goose Rhymes*
1914	*Handy Pandy and Other Mother Goose Rhymes*
1914	*Jumping Joan and Other Mother Goose Rhymes*
1914	*Little Jenny Wren and Other Mother Goose Rhymes*
1916	*Jack and Jill and Other Mother Goose Rhymes*

Double-sided books by Sarah Cory Rippey. Chicago: Rand McNally.

1913	*The Goody-Naughty Book*
1915	*The Sunny-Sulky Book*

The Goosey Goosey Gander series. Chicago: Rand McNally.

1916	*Polly Flinders*
1916	*Tommy Tittlemouse*
1917	*Little Jack Horner*

Jolly Mother Goose. Chicago: Rand McNally, 1916.

Little Brothers to the Scouts by E. A. Watson Hyde. Chicago: Rand McNally, 1917.

The Natural Method Readers; A Second Reader by Hannah T. McManus and John H. Haaren. New York: Charles Scribner's Sons, 1915.

The Real Mother Goose. Chicago: Rand McNally, 1916.

Dada

Dada is nonsense. Dada is chance. Dada is play.

Dada is creating art with humor and absurdity to challenge what many people might think is right or normal.

Dada is a movement started by a group of artists and writers in Zurich, Switzerland, in 1916 who were horrified by the brutality and stupidity of World War I. These artists and writers figured their nonsense made better sense than killing millions of people.

Dada artists goofed around with painting, writing, sculpture, music, photography, performance art, and puppets. Dada artists cut up and reassembled everyday objects, printed materials, and images to make new art.

One of the most famous pieces of Dada art is by Marcel Duchamp. He took a cheap postcard of the Mona Lisa and drew a mustache and a goatee on it.

The Dada movement quickly spread to other cities—Berlin, Paris, New York, Cologne. It inspired many artists. It inspired many more art movements.

No one knows exactly where the name Dada came from. Some say it was picked randomly from a French/German dictionary. Others say it was meant to sound like a baby's first word. Others say it was for "Yes, yes" in Russian. In this way Dada is like nothing, and also like everything.

And that all sounds perfectly Dada deep nonsense right.

For more Dada fun, look up Hugo Ball, Hannah Höch, Francis Picabia, Marcel Duchamp, Kurt Schwitters, Hans Arp, Sophie Taeuber-Arp, Raoul Hausmann, and Max Ernst.

And please make some Dada fun of your own.